Herbie's

HAPPY BIRTHDAY

**Athena Phillips
and
Donte' Jackson**

**Herbie Vore the Dinosaur
Book 1**

**Illustrated by
Meredith Mills**

HERBIE'S HAPPY BIRTHDAY!
Herbie Vore the Dinosaur series, Book 1

ISBN: 978-0-692-10358-6

Book and cover design by Sarah Holroyd
(https://sleepingcatbooks.com)

This book is dedicated to my grandmother, "Maw Maw" Frances Phillips, who always made our birthdays very special!

    Love, Athena

To my beloved grandparents Katherine and Joseph Jackson, thank you for always believing in me.

    Donte'

For my Nana and Papa, Shirley and Mike McClearn. Your endless support has made this whole adventure possible.

    I love you, Meredith

Today is a special one for little Herbie Vore.
He jumped up from his bed ready to explore.

Herbie's mother Alice and his father Ted
Were waiting when the birthday boy hurried out of bed.

"Happy Birthday Herbie!" they yelled.
He greeted them with excitement.
Pancakes he smelled!

4

Herbie ate all of his pancakes while smiling with joy. "Are my friends coming soon? I can't wait! Oh, boy!"

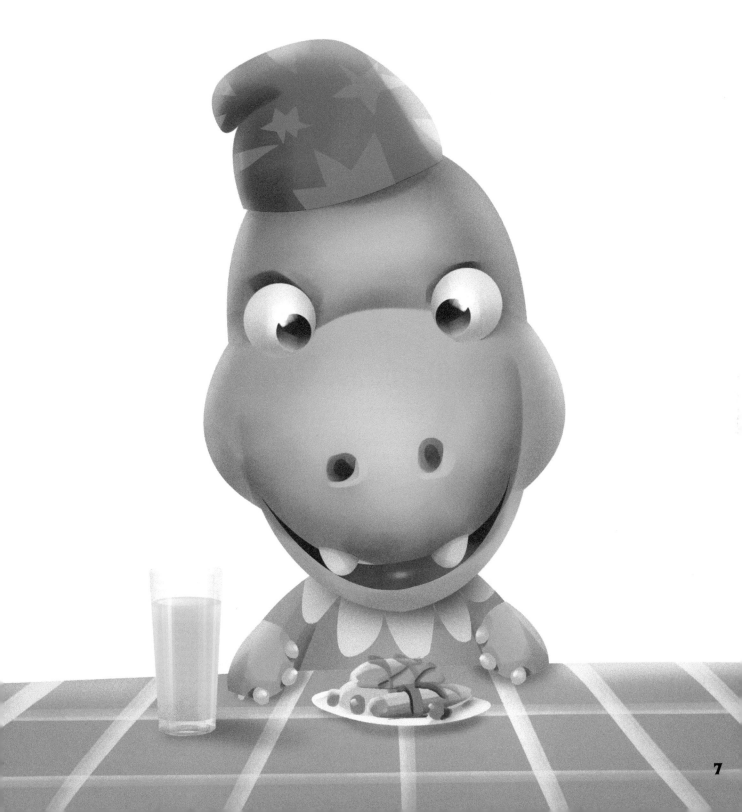

Happy Birthday, Hooray!
Today is Herbie's special day.

I had better dress up and look nice for my guests.
But what should I wear on my birthday?
A vest!

Herbie got dressed and
tried on different hats...

Cowboy hat, firefighter, yellow duck cap?

Aha! My birthday hat...at last!

**Herbie helped his Grandma Martha decorate the house.
"Oh, look who's early, my little buddy Mouse!"**

Soon, Herbie's other friends started to come in.
Balloons filled the room! Now the party begins!

Herbie's best friends were there to celebrate.
"Let's play some games before it gets too late!"

Happy Birthday, Hooray!
Today is Herbie's special day.

They pinned the tail on the dino and played musical chairs Heidi hit the pinata—candy flew everywhere!

Look!
Strawberries, ice cream, birthday cake and more.
Such yummy special treats for a growing Herbie Vore.

Herbie's friends gathered around
And sang "Happy Birthday"
Oh, what a festive sound!

26

Herbie blew out his candles and made a birthday wish.
He said, "Let's take a picture, everybody squish!"

Herbie and his friends enjoyed the frosted cake.
Grandma said, "Don't eat too much, you'll get a bellyache!"

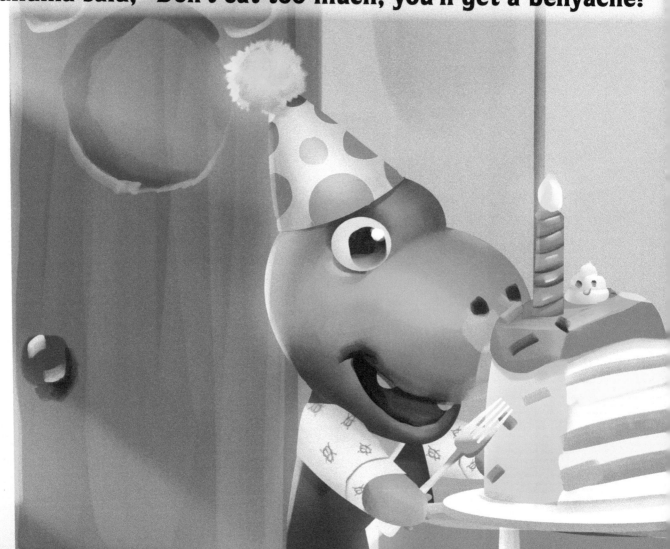

Then it was time for presents, how fun!
Herbie unwrapped books and a hat.
"Wow! Thank you, everyone!"

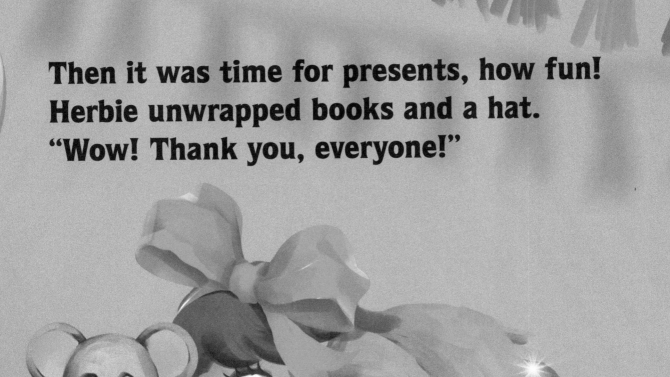

The party was almost over
He wished it wouldn't end.
Herbie waved a quick goodbye,
Best wishes to his friends.

Happy Birthday, Hooray!
Today is Herbie's special day.

"Momma, why is my birthday just one time each year?"

38

"If birthdays came 'round more than one time a year, your special day would lose its good cheer."

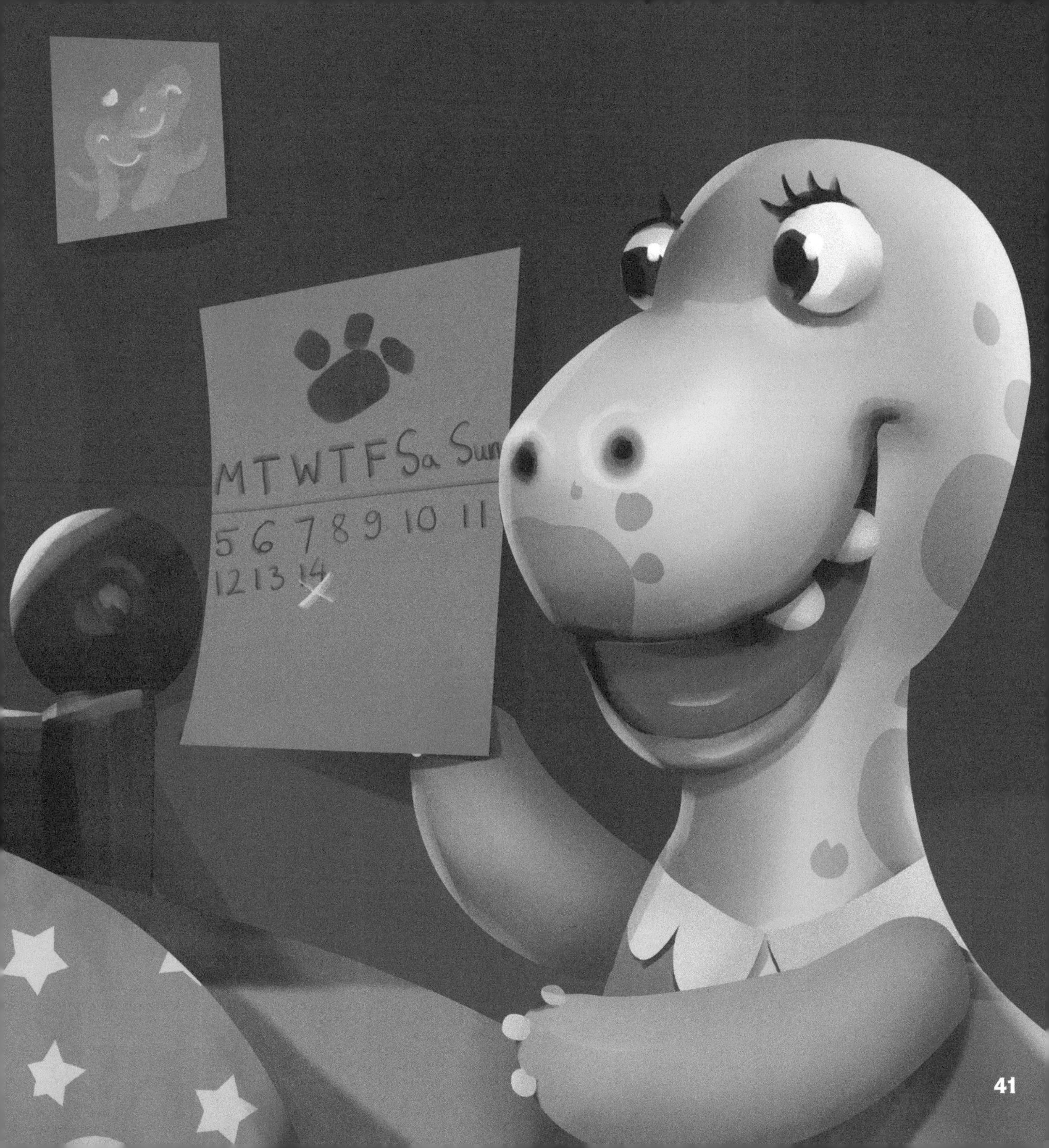
M T W T F Sa Sun
5 6 7 8 9 10 11
12 13 14

Herbie put away his gifts and climbed back into bed
After his new picture book had already been read.
Herbie's mom turned off the light
Blew him a kiss and hugged Herbie tight.

Happy birthday, dear Herbie,
Have sweet dreams tonight.

Goodnight, Herbie Vore the Dinosaur!

Athena Phillips is an author, English teacher, and part-time children's librarian. Her dream to author children's books began while earning her graduate degree at Belmont University in Nashville, Tennessee. A resident of Franklin, Tennessee, Athena collaborated with Donte' Jackson to bring Herbie Vore the Dinosaur's world to life in her first published book, **Herbie's Happy Birthday!** When she's not writing one of Herbie's adventures, Athena enjoys traveling to magical lands such as Austria, Budapest and Prague.

Donte' Jackson is a painter, poet, writer, part-time philosopher and resident of Southern California. He specializes in character design and story development, and the concept for the world of Herbie Vore the Dinosaur was born in his imagination. His other projects include comic books and movie scripts. In his spare time, Donte' enjoys reading and watching documentaries, movies and cartoons. All of his creative endeavors originate from his extensive study of the metaphysical.

Meredith is a freelance illustrator currently living in Southern California. She has been drawing since she was a toddler and now uses her graphic design skills to create whimsical animal characters that kids connect with and love. Meredith was born and raised in Nashville, Tennessee, and moved to Los Angeles in 2016 to begin pursuing her career in art. When she's not illustrating Herbie Vore and his friends, Meredith enjoys reading, playing video games, making music, and babysitting. Like Herbie Vore, she also collects hats!

Parents and teachers: your kids can have fun with Herbie online at Herbievore.com.

CPSIA information can be obtained
at www.ICGtesting.com
Printed in the USA
BVHW02*2325130918
527316BV00002B/3/P

9 780692 103586